THE QUANGLE WANGLE'S HAT

by Edward Lear

Pictures by

Helen Oxenbury

First published in Great Britain 1969
by William Heinemann Ltd
Published 1994 by Mammoth
an imprint of Egmont Children's Books Limited
239 Kensington High St
London W8 6SA
Reprinted 1995. Reissued 1999
10 9 8 7 6 5 4 3 2

For John

Illustrations copyright © Helen Oxenbury 1969
ISBN 0 7497 1336 4

A CIP catalogue record for this title is available from the British Library

Printed in the U.A.E. by Oriental Press

On top of the Crumpetty Tree

The Quangle Wangle sat,

But his face you could not see,

On account of his Beaver Hat.

For his Hat was a hundred and two feet wide,

With ribbons and bibbons on every side,

And bells, and buttons, and loops, and lace,

So that nobody ever could see the face

Of the Quangle Wangle Quee.

The Quangle Wangle said

To himself on the Crumpetty Tree:

"Jam; and jelly; and bread;

Are the best of food for me!

But the longer I live on this Crumpetty Tree,
The plainer than ever it seems to me
That very few people come this way,
And that life on the whole is far from gay!"
Said the Quangle Wangle Quee.

But there came to the Crumpetty Tree

Mr. and Mrs. Canary;

And they said, "Did ever you see

Any spot so charmingly airy?

May we build a nest on your lovely Hat?
Mr. Quangle Wangle, grant us that!
O please let us come and build a nest
Of whatever material suits you best,
Mr. Quangle Wangle Quee!"

And besides, to the Crumpetty Tree
Came the Stork, the Duck, and the Owl;
The Snail and the Bumble-Bee,

The Frog, and the Fimble Fowl

(The Fimble Fowl with a corkscrew leg);

And all of them said, "We humbly beg,

We may build our homes on your lovely Hat,

Mr. Quangle Wangle, grant us that!

Mr. Quangle Wangle Quee!"

And the Golden Grouse came there,
And the Pobble who has no toes,

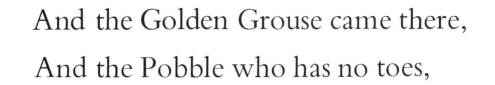

And the small Olympian bear

And the Dong with a luminous nose

the Blue Baboon, who played the flute,

And the Orient Calf from the Land of Tute,

And the Attery Squash

and the Bisky Bat,

All came and built on the lovely Hat
Of the Quangle Wangle Quee.

And the Quangle Wangle said
To himself on the Crumpetty Tree,
"When all these creatures move
What a wonderful noise there'll be!"

And at night by the light of the Mulberry Moon
They danced to the Flute of the Blue Baboon
On the broad green leaves of the Crumpetty Tree,
And all were as happy as happy could be,

With the Quangle Wangle Quee.